STANDARD CANDLE

G.B. Lindsey

By the Author

Novellas
One Door Closes (book 1 of *Secrets of Neverwood*)
Out With the Old

• • • •

Anthologies
Secrets of Neverwood: An Anthology
Condoms and Hot Tubs Don't Mix: An Anthology of Awkward Sexcapades
Best Lesbian Erotica of the Year, Volume 5

G.B. LINDSEY

THE HOUSE IS FULL, and cars clutter the street at strange angles from the curb. Hot air buffets when you open the door. Sweat, alcohol—the odor curls at your guts. Someone inside has weed. Denny pushes in, dragging you in his slipstream between bumping bodies, through slurred shouts. You haul on the hem of his jacket and lean close enough to smell his cologne.

"Remember the deal?" But the music vibrates down into your throat. It's hard to tell if Denny heard you.

You and Denny have a deal, designed while buzzed, agreed upon while drunk, and enacted every time the roulette comes up zero. Sometimes, you go home with someone else. Sometimes, you go home with Denny. But you never go home alone.

You fuck, plain and simple. It's good—really good. Denny's got a couple of long-term relationships under his belt, you were engaged to someone once before it just didn't make sense anymore, and you both know your way around a one-night stand. You've got a heinous talent for blow jobs, and Den's a fucking ace at... well, fucking.

You haven't bottomed for anyone else, but Denny doesn't know that.

Tonight, Denny smells like leather. He owns one jacket—his father's—dirty brown and skinned at the elbows. On work mornings, he stumbles out of his bed and into a frayed cotton tee covered with oil stains. In jeans, always. Tonight, a pine-green shirt peers out from under his collar. It turns his eyes into beacons.

You met through older siblings, which is hilarious, seeing as your sister disowned you and Denny hasn't spoken to his brother since Stewart married a fundamentalist woman and converted. Fundamentalist something. What kind of fundamentalism was it, anyway? You wonder if Stewart holds a sign now and protests in infuriating ways.

But before all that, your sister and his brother went to college together, and they held a kegger—your first, age sixteen, and there was this obscenely drunk, obscenely chatty high school senior with one hand on your nape as you threw up your guts in the backyard, who told you—

"Don't drink the punch at these things." Denny slaps your side and rubs it once, already looking away.

"I know."

You lived an isolated existence back then. And then you lived for Denny Wyatt. Other people were around; there are other humans on this earth after all. But from that party on, Denny was always there—birthdays, groundings, graduation. Somehow constantly at the center of it all. Maybe you were circling him all that time, a satellite orbiting a planet, but the difference was that this planet circled back. Twin stars stalking each other, sharing their stellar matter as the years passed by, never the same as it was a month prior, but one thing always was: Den was your best friend.

And now, even that's different.

"Andy!" Someone grabs you, and then begin the back slaps, hand slaps. Hugs that bump and bruise. "College boy!"

Den's actually the college boy between the two of you, but this guy slapping your back lives in his parents' ranch-style two neighborhoods over, throws their money around while calling it his, and takes his car to Denny for upkeep. He won't care that the Denny Wyatt he knows—the one who wears stained shirts and fixes a rich boy's Trans Am when the engine coughs shit all over the road—once also tried for a degree.

"My name's Avery," you say.

"What?"

"Avery. Not Andy."

The Trans Am guy smiles and shrugs, palms to the ceiling. "Sorry, man."

Denny's a year and a half older than you. He went to college for three semesters. Den's a science guy, the smartest you know, but the labs took up too much of his week and the rent on his room was always, always coming up late. You watched him start course after course—O-Chem, Anatomy and Physiology, Microbiology—only to drop it halfway through, promising to take it up again when he had money saved up, when next semester rolled around. After three *next semester*s, he gave up. You stayed on, got your associate, and then couldn't find anything to do with it except transfer to a four-year and go so far into debt, you'd never get out—and that was assuming you landed those scholarships on top of it all.

You loathed those applications. You got drunk and punched Denny in the face over the University of California set the night before they were due, got punched back, kicked him out of your house, and then sent the applications off anyway because you felt bad about Denny's jaw. When you told him the next day, the two of you with matching bruises on your cheeks, he gave you an uneven smile and informed you that you were coming out drinking with him. You weren't even twenty. Denny bought you beer until you found one with a flavor you liked, and the two of you got drunk enough to forget why you'd done it in the first place.

You didn't get the scholarships.

Trans Am bumps your shoulder and forgets you arrived, but Denny has long since woven away through the crowd, giving real hugs to tipsy, laughing people.

He's always been able to hug.

And smile. He makes enough with that smile to keep his room—first as a waiter and then cleaning exam rooms for the town veterinarian. Now he's managing an auto shop, which leaves his skin smelling like motor oil. It would make a good blurb on the back cover of a novel if Denny ever wrote about it. Writers have the weirdest jobs. But Denny's spelling still kind of sucks, and he couldn't care less about dangling participles. His current coworkers are in the tiny little party circuit downtown, and the auto shop closes at five, so Denny's always free, and you're always willing to go with him. You don't have anything else to do. You have a hard time having a good time when Denny's not there.

There's a giant Jenga in the middle of the kitchen table that goes over when you walk in, landing on someone's foot.

"Fuck! Fuck, you asshole!" the guy shouts at the room and staggers into the pantry, upsetting packs of spaghetti on the shelves.

You get yourself a beer from a couple of girls sprawled on their stomachs across the marble bar top. One of them waits tables with you at a place in the city twenty minutes out, where half of the staff sings arias—this woman breaks crystal wine glasses with her high Cs—and every week, there's an octogenarian who pats your ass when you're trying to put in their dinner order.

"Hey, Avery," your coworker says, waving. The bangles on her wrist skitter like insects.

"Hey, Maxine."

Maxine is all dark hair and nice curves. Somehow, she still makes worse tips than you do, even from the perverts. You make pretty good tips, except that Denny borrows them to buy his cigarettes.

"Tainted money, Ave," he always says. "You wouldn't feel right spending it."

He always pays you back in auto repairs, and he doesn't take your griping seriously anymore. Maybe if you sounded less whiny, he'd do more than nod along to your nicotine tirade.

You tell him you hate how his cigarettes smell. It's a little bit of a lie; you don't really hate anything associated with him.

But even with Denny's sticky fingers, you make enough to keep your half of the little duplex on Belmont Circle, right next to a workaholic thirty-something you only see when she dashes out to her car at god-awful o'clock, high heels clacking down the walk. Her name is Serena; you never got her last name. Next door is Mr. Abbott, who is slowly letting his house go to seed and himself along with it. His daughters have three kids each and keep trying to put him in a home.

He's lonely, which makes him hateful, which makes him cruel, and he stares at you like you tore out all his crabgrass and stuffed it into his mailbox in the middle of the night. Your own front lawn is a mess, and the walkway up to your door is cracked practically in half; your landlord does jack shit about any of it. You dream of joining forces with Serena one day—she's a paralegal, you think—and finally getting your rent's worth, but until then, it's good to get out of your place and into someone else's. Get plastered with Denny. Get laid in a comfortable bed. Sometimes, it's Denny's bed, his neighbors throwing a garden party out back like they're upwardly mobile instead of stuck living in the Clovis cul-de-sac, and it's nice to just lie there in a daze afterward, naked as a baby, and not worry about someone rifling through your jeans while you sleep, looking for your wallet.

Denny always asks first.

This party is full of weed you don't smoke and liquor you don't drink, but the atmosphere makes you high—thumping rave music, people wearing half the clothing they arrived in, and black lights in a revamped Victorian that has industrial chic piping in the kitchen. So fucking wrong. Denny knows the host, a friend of a friend of his boss; turns out, this friend of a friend is forty-five with a permanent leer and a bead on some big-city Molly.

But this is a small town, and there are tons of people here tonight who aren't from here. You only recognize half of the faces, and you just want to let go for the night. Watch Trans Am head for YouTube infamy by trying to shuffle in the middle of the living room. Stick by Denny's side until you find someone to go home with.

Denny surveys faces in the crowd like they're answering specific questions for him. There's a space of three feet between the two of you all evening, which is more space than usual. You make fun of Trans Am. Denny cups his ear until you repeat it and then laughs a little. And finally, he ends up on the other side of the crowd by the stereo, his beat-up jacket hugging his frame as he flips through CDs.

You freak dance with two girls, one Maxine and one by accident, before you have to get out of the way of the second one's boyfriend—this big, beefy frat boy who takes one look at you and sneers, then takes a second look and lets you go.

You're tall, and you've got muscles, but truthfully, you're not a fighter. You're not fond of confrontation. You remind yourself of the mastiff mix your stepdad had when you were a kid—as big as a pony but gentle as a bunny. When you walked that dog, people would see you coming and cross the street. Denny's scrappier, smaller than you, but people don't mess around with him. They don't even try. You've wanted to know his secret since the night you met him.

Denny checks out sometime around eleven. You realize it too late to do anything about it. More people pour in from the only club downtown. The air gets thicker and smokier and the partiers get drunker. You start feeling as though you have stepped outside yourself and are looking in, staring at this uneasy, overgrown kid in the middle of a mob of screwed up adults.

Who did Denny leave with? If he left with anybody. All you have is his voice in your ear, not quite loud enough, the squeeze of his hand on your arm. You come to yourself and look at your watch; it's 11:16, and Denny is gone. The house is packed. The house feels empty. Dancing immediately becomes a chore. You peer over the tops of heads, unable to stop searching for him even though you know he's no longer there.

Eventually, it's past midnight, and you're halfway home with Maxine, your coworker from the opera bar, when you admit to yourself that you don't want to be with her tonight. Your body does—hell yeah, it does. But the click doesn't come, that last little sidestep where the night goes from idiotic to ingenious. Maxine's wearing a short black sheath that barely covers the tops of her thighs. You imagine sliding the straps off her shoulders, unzipping the dress, slipping it down her hips, and your stomach rolls like you ate a chunk of that black mold you saw on the porch at the party. What you want to do is talk, but not to her; none of it will make any sense to her, and that's when the night slots down, thuds deep in your gut, heads in a completely different direction.

You have no idea how you didn't see this before, because it's big, and it's scary as hell; it feels like it's always been lurking there, letting you catch glimpses out of the corner of your eye. You *recognize* it. You've seen it before, but you never—*never*—knew what it was you were looking at. It's hard to breathe.

You pull the truck over to the side of the road and listen to your passenger's confusion.

"What's wrong? Are you okay?"

"Maxine, where do you live?"

"You want to go to my house?"

You stare out the windshield, grip and regrip the wheel, and don't answer.

She looks at you narrowly across the truck's cab. Her makeup is smudged, making her eyes large and smoky. "Are you serious?"

She gets it. She's mad.

Answering is too much to ask of yourself right now. Your memories of yourself, of Denny, are re-layering. You're standing waist deep in an ocean and being hit with wave upon wave until it's all you can do to stay upright. You flail in the undertow, your mouth full of salt, and when you finally find your feet again, you can only look back at her and nod. Just nod and breathe sweet, sweet air. It's coming down off a mountain. You taste more and more oxygen in every lungful, feeding each starving cell.

She shakes her head and throws a hand out. "Fine. Just turn right."

You turn the truck onto the road again, rapidly tapping your fingers. You can't keep them still anymore.

She directs you in curt syllables to a two-story townhouse in the new development and slams your door without saying good night. She doesn't deserve to be ditched like this. You stare after her, hoping she'll still talk to you at work, and then she's inside and you turn around, cross to the other side of town, head to Denny's place.

It's quiet out. A few porchlights are on, mostly in the tiny apartment complex. Denny's is one of them. His stoop is plain and flat, just a concrete slab with a railing, a single potted plant at the edge. The broken step is fixed, filled in with barely smoothed cement, and the old screen door has finally been replaced.

When you knock, the front door opens. Den looks bewildered, still in the jeans he wore to the party, the dark lines hugging his legs and washing out to thundercloud blue at the knees. His green shirt's off, just a thin, ribbed tank top. "Avery?"

"Hey." The sight of him shoves core deep. You want *this*. You don't need any more parties or deals.

Denny knows your real first name—Grayson; what were your parents thinking?—and that you go by your middle name instead. He knows why you can't stand pistachio ice cream. He stood there and listened to you curse every gay person in existence when you were seventeen and stupid, parroting your parents, your friendship only six months old.

He cleaned up your hand when you broke the window of your truck, the same night you owned up to liking guys, and then again when your sister, Julianna, called you, screaming in your ear that being bisexual was *"a choice you made, Avery, don't ever call me again!"*

Denny knows how uncertain you were about kissing another guy, how anticlimactic your first time having sex was, and how you were too unsettled to admit you'd been with a guy at all. Denny knows about those three dismal months when you decided he'd turned you gay and told him so every time he came over, calling him every name in the book except faggot because you couldn't get it out, couldn't ever call him *that*. Denny watched you break, listened to you beg. He knows how you sound when you are sorrier than you ever thought it was possible to be.

Denny knows how to fuck you right through your orgasm and out the other side, until all you see is white and blue, and it never ends. Never feels like it's going to end.

Denny blinks under the light of the porch bulb. His hair, done up in spikes for the party, is now ruffled and flat. His fingers are a beautiful curl around the door's frame. Singular. Steady. You could pick them out of a lineup. You want to take them in your hands, link them with your fingers, spell Den's name out across his palm with the tip of your thumb.

"Thought you were with Maxine Whitaker." His voice breaks through your bubble, and you meet his eyes.

Was he still there after all? Did he see you leave with her?

Like always, you reorient by watching him. Denny has the deepest brown eyes of anyone, almost black when he's excited. His brows are low, drawn together, not a trace of irritation. God, he's perfect.

"Den, you ever—"

You've never felt like you couldn't talk to him; there has never been so much crowding through your airways and thoughts all at once. But, even with all that, you're still going to speak. Because he's Denny. There's no shame in asking for his help. He'll listen to all of it, no matter what it is, and together, you'll figure it out. You always have.

"You ever felt like you just suddenly ... *get it*? Everything. That it all makes perfect sense? And you were a complete moron not to have seen it."

Denny knows you're a moron. Knows you think of yourself as a moron anyway. He gets this look in his eye when you say it out loud though, and it's the same look as now—that glint of dispute. But you don't want to argue that tonight. You wave your hands, trying to encompass it all in one tangible *thing* that Denny can touch and see. Of course, that's impossible. You don't even know the right words to convey the magnitude of this epiphany and what it's done to you.

You're happy. It's not a feeling you're familiar with. With your high school girlfriend, Jude—Judith to her parents—you felt like this. It was so long ago, you forget sometimes, but tonight you remember the sensation. Feeling whole, like there's nothing in the world that could possibly improve your situation, and everything's laid out like a relief map of where you've been and which road you're heading down. All the mountainous peaks and the curving rivers arrow to the place you will ultimately end up. Tonight, it makes perfect sense that Denny is responsible.

Denny stares at you with his mouth open, eyes flicking along with the motion of your hands. He lets out a laugh. Short, like a breath. "Can't say I have, Ave. Are you okay?"

You're not. And you *are.* You want to touch his shirt, smooth the fabric between your fingers, feel the heat of his skin underneath. And, well, why not? So, you reach; you brush his shoulder with your knuckles. Holy hell, you know his smell, all of it. The whole apartment smells like Denny, even the tiny little stoop, oily and tart and prickly and warm. The scent tosses up memories in its wake, snapshots, snatches of thought, some of them just feelings. It's staggering how much you managed to miss when it was with you all along.

Denny catches your hands but doesn't push, just holds you still. "Ave, really, are you—"

You grip him tight, and it's just like every other time, only fuller, heavier than stripped clothing and sex. You want to kiss him. Push him inside his apartment and lay him out on his dingy couch and show him how perfect you know he is.

"Den, you're always here, and now I ... see it. I'm not saying this right. Are you—can I—"

You don't actually care if you do this on Denny's front porch, a revelation for all the world to witness. But Den might care. Den has to live here with these people, in this complex.

Inside, outside, wherever. You just need to be here with him.

Denny's hands fall from yours. He steadies himself on the doorframe. He's baffled and curious, and a little closed off. That last expression is an oddly familiar one, and you don't remember registering it before, but you have seen it. Recently and often.

"I—" He stops and looks back over his shoulder into the apartment. His fingers clench on the frame, a little shiver, and suddenly you get it.

He's got someone there.

It cuts into your chest. You didn't connect the dots. He's half-undressed, and it hurts. So much. It's air you don't have—a deal you took for granted, an understanding stabbed right through in one shiny thrust.

Denny's not a dater. He's not. He sleeps with people, but he doesn't take them back home; he doesn't hand out glasses of wine or bags of chips, and they don't sit on the couch next to him and shoot the shit. They certainly don't wait in unseen recesses of his living room while he shoos unwelcome friends off the front porch.

You can't move, can't even react when Denny steps closer. He speaks, probably your name, but your brain is a muddle, still trying to find the thread you lost track of, and that's why you're still standing there when Michael Armstrong walks into the front hall, barefoot.

You thought you knew pain before, but it is nothing, *nothing* compared to this. You know this guy. Mike. You've met him, and he's okay—tall, scraggly-thin, plays a mean bass when he's high. One of Denny's exes, the amiable breakup. The one Den gets the quietest over. Preschool playmate, best friend before you, high school brother in arms. Lover. Loved.

"I'm sor—" You step back and trip down the steps, almost falling, but instinct locks your hand around the iron railing.

Denny follows onto the stoop, but you hold your hands up, a wall between you. The space is a chasm.

"Sorry, I didn't realize." That's all you've got. You turn, feet taking you away, muscles humming under the assault. Your body knows Denny. Remembers Denny inside it and around it, all over it. Strangely, your body also suddenly recalls the feel of Denny grabbing your phone, the satisfying yank when you took it back, the smell of spilled alcohol and the pure hatred over a specific phone number that he begged you to erase from your Contacts.

"Don't call her. Don't put yourself through that."

"You're telling me what to do?"

"Avery, do not call your sister again!"

You recall how it felt to break your phone against the wall, to nearly break your hand. You remember the burn of the ice pack afterward and how cold his fingers felt when he pressed them to your bare side. You remember hating yourself because you were responsible for that ugly glower on his face. You remember pushing him down into his bed for the first time of many, rocking against him, panting into his mouth. You remember finally shifting the blame for your grief to your sister where it belonged, instead of on yourself or on him. That moment has nothing to do with this moment, but suddenly, it's the one you remember.

God, you need him. You are so gone for him, but you've been an idiot. Always a fool until it's way past too late, always missing the throw and regretting it when the ball's gone by into someone else's glove.

Mike has a lifetime with Den, a childhood and a slew of schools; long before you, he was wrapping his arm around Den's shoulders, coaxing him through heartbreak and congratulating his successes. He gave Denny a place to stay when he finally ditched his parents and their Bible-thumping delusions. Mike and Denny have years on you and Den—and not just as friends.

You have a failed engagement, a photo album full of regrets, a family you barely talk to, but this pain is fresh and deep and different. Your body isn't ready to regret this yet; your mind is still screaming from the blow.

You love Denny. And that should be something. You're *in love* with him, down deep, and you never saw it for what it was. You've wrenched your own insides apart. You're bleeding in there where no one can see.

You don't remember getting into your truck. It's a beat-up single cab with a sticky driver's door and a transmission that still runs when the key falls out, but you don't recall turning the ignition or driving. You do remember headlights, a horn blaring, a light turning red before you're ready. Somehow, you end up at home in one piece, parked at the curb with the truck's cabin growing cold around you.

Whenever Denny rides shotgun, he angles his body into the corner so he can face you when he talks. He props his left knee on the bench and shoves his seat belt down under both arms, even when you yell at him about it slipping between his ribs and cutting him in half if there were an accident.

Tonight, the cabin is empty, dark. You hear the absence of his laughter as though it, too, has a sound, living and breathing long after the laugh itself is silenced.

You drop your face into your hands. You should have kissed him there, on his stoop, just so you could have that one last time.

When did you fall? You didn't trip over it or happen upon it. Were you in his bed, getting fucked against the headboard, pinching his tongue between your teeth and enjoying the flavor, or were you sitting on his couch, tossing bell peppers and pepperoni at his head while he tried to find the game on TV? Maybe your body knew it before your mind caught up. You've always been drawn to him; maybe being in love has always been why.

You want him to be yours, more than you ever wanted Jude, even when you wanted to marry her. You want to possess Denny, and you know it's wrong, but you want to rule his heart and his thoughts, be there each time he dreams and breathes, every time he closes his eyes. He doesn't belong to you. He doesn't belong to anyone, and your possessiveness is irrational, but you *know* that Mike Armstrong has heard the way Den's voice cracks during sex, the way he breathes his lover's name on the crest of coming. You don't want anyone else to know those sounds, but maybe it's even worse than that. Maybe Mike has already heard a voice Denny's never shared with you.

You feel the rift as something lasting inside you breaks. All you want to do is shut your eyes and forget.

You and Denny fuck. It's plain. Simple. A series of one-night stands. Even if you once made love to him by accident, there's no guarantee he ever did the same to you.

A dull thumping reaches your ears.

"Avery."

Denny stands on the other side of the window, his palm pressed flat against the glass. He says your name again, muffled, in a tone that tells you he's been calling you for a while.

How long has he been there?

"Avery, open the door!"

You do, but it's not a conscious thought, just an instinctive response to his voice. And that response, too, is familiar.

Denny reaches in before the door is completely open and hauls you out by your jacket, his fists twisted in the fabric. He pulls until he's got you in his arms, wrapped in a hug you never saw coming.

Then he shoves you away, hard.

"What the hell were you doing?" Denny knocks your shoulder forcefully enough to send you back against the side of your truck. "What the hell, Avery?"

You don't even know what the question is. Everything's as raw as a fresh burn.

"Are you high? You drunk?"

"Den."

He glares at you, jaw tight. He looks so much more alive than you feel, and it shrivels your nerves, leaves them brittle.

"What is wrong with you? You show up in the middle of the night not making any sense, and then you almost get wiped out by a fucking Hummer? You weren't even wearing a seat belt. What the *fuck*, Ave?" The tremor in his voice is sobering. You've never seen him so disturbed.

"I'm fine." You try swallowing. "I'm fine."

He takes you by the shoulders and tips you back until you bump the truck again, and then he holds you there. His jacket smells like his cigarettes—faint and, again, comforting. You've been trying and failing not to take comfort in that for ages.

"Your phone's off. You look like you saw a fucking ghost." His eyes widen, and he leans back, checks the truck, the front bumper, the side panels. "Did you—did someone—"

You shake your head. He's squeezing you too tightly. It hurts.

Still he searches, peering at you so intently, you feel like he's scraping out your insides, seeing everything there is to see.

Finally, he sighs. Cups your *cheek*. "What's wrong? Talk to me, man."

You can't. None of the things you want to say will answer that question without the help of a lengthy explanation. And you don't have one.

You want him so badly, even now. Especially now. You want to wrap your arms around him and touch the hot flutter at his throat with your tongue. You want to press your mouths together, drink him up like syrup, shape the sounds he makes with your own lips. You want to open him up, ease inside, feel every inch, and you want to do it *knowing* what you feel for him this time, tasting the mortality of it in your mouth, the finite, dangerous heat of what Denny does to you, is to you.

It makes you so helpless, you could cry, that all you have is twenty-twenty hindsight and an understanding well after the moment of action.

"Ave, is your family all right?" Denny looks frantic now. He thinks that's the only thing that could mess you up so badly—something happening to your family. In spite of all they've done to you and all you've put him through over it, he goes there first.

You choke on a laugh. He doesn't even imagine that he could cause this break in you, that he's that important.

God, why couldn't you have known sooner, so you could have told him how much he was always worth to you?

"It's not.... My family's fine."

He's still pressing you against the truck, like you'll run if he lets you go.

You reach and then lower your hands without touching. "It's me. Just ... this is my fault."

He tightens his grip on your jacket. His thumb drifts against your cheek, and you want his hand off your face because it's too much of what you need. He doesn't know what he's giving you.

"Avery." A statement. "Are you hurt? Someone hurt you?"

That final question hardens in such a way that you almost do cry. If you said the word, Den would find whoever harmed you and pummel the shit out of them. He'd go right now, like he went for your stepdad after the fight last Christmas and you barely caught up and stopped him in time. But this time, either you've hurt yourself or he's the one who did it, and you don't want to see him beat himself up for something he can't control.

"I'm okay. I swear."

"You're not," Denny fires back.

It's then, right then, that you realize you're going to tell him. He knows how you lie, particularly when you lie to him. He'll see it in an instant—he's probably already seen it—and he never stops until he has the truth out of you.

Usually it feels like lancing a wound. You can't imagine what this will feel like.

"Just want you happy," you say. That's the biggest understatement on earth, and you know you're completely screwed now.

You want Denny to never hurt, to be happy, like he deserves. And how could you make him happy? You can't commit. You complain and yell and fight him. You use him for nights when you can't get dates. You don't even know it when you're falling in love.

You can't remember the last time he *really* smiled because of something you did.

"Avery—"

"He makes you better."

Denny's face twists. "Who does?"

You can say his name. It's just a name. "Mike."

You don't blame Denny for his confusion; you're not making much sense. Is there a way to acknowledge Denny's good fortune without giving away how much it devastates you? Would you even know how to articulate that?

"What about Mike?" His fingers are still on your face.

You don't know what to say next. Wish Den joy? It'll ring false. Tell him you're sorry? He'll just ask why. You should have kept driving.

"Avery." Denny grasps your shoulders and shakes you. You must be coming across as completely insane by now. "If you don't give me an answer right now, so help me God—"

The crack widens, and you're already off-balance. You sway and grab Denny's arms. He catches you at the waist and pulls you back upright.

Someone is saying, "I'm sorry, I'm sorry," and you realize it's you.

"Hey, come here. C'mere." Denny cups the back of your neck and tucks you in until the two of you are breathing the same air. He's warm all over. He smells like beer from the party, cigarette smoke, oil, burning rice husks, an autumn scent. Everything. "God, Ave, what's wrong?"

His lips shape the words right against your ear. He pulls back, takes your face in both hands, and brushes the corner of your mouth with a kiss.

"Den, wait."

You don't know if you mean to push him away or pull him in. You just know you can't stop yourself anymore. You meet his mouth again, sweet and quick. Again, longer. Again, trying to taste him, to tell him what he is to you in a simple kiss. But it's no longer simple; you're moving with it, your whole body rocking up into it, threading your fingers into his hair, pushing his mouth open until his jaw goes slack and his flavor blows wide over your tongue. You need this, just once more. If he's really ... *really* getting back with Mike. You've never felt so desperate. So cognizant of how Denny makes you tick.

He tries for air, and you let him. Then you take him back, and it's even better, even worse. His hands fist, digging into your shoulder blades, just holding on, and it feels like what you're trying to do, trying to hold on for one more second.

He pulls out of it with a rasp, and you know it's over.

"Ave." He pants more than speaks, eyes hooded and blown black. You can see how swollen his lips are in the light from the sodium lamps, and the words spill from you, squeezed by the fist of impending loss.

"Don't hate me, Den. Please don't hate me. I need you, I don't want anyone else. I really don't know what's wrong with me—"

His eyes flick over your face, like some other explanation is there if he can just find it. He's gripping you too tightly again. The bite of it is sharp.

"Denny, I'm not what you need, and I'm sorry."

His face shivers, lips and eyelids contracting; even his nostrils flare. His jaw quivers with strain, and somewhere deep down, you're afraid.

"Fuck you, Avery," he hisses. His fingers lift and drop down again on your back, his hold reaffirmed. You watch his mouth curl around a snarl that makes him look like someone else entirely. "*Fuck* you."

The whisper is worse than a cry. What's more, it's broken, and the look in his eyes says you broke it. He gives you a little shake. His eyes are wet.

You reach without thinking, to touch just beneath his eye, and he jerks back like you clubbed him.

"Den. Den, I'm sorry."

His hand drops from where he's holding you. The cold air burns.

"You don't know what I need." He shakes his head from side to side, like he can't believe what he's looking at, and steps away.

"He's good for you." You choke it out. You have to.

Denny stares at you like you told him you were dying, or that he was.

"Who—shut *up,* Avery!"

He's not touching you; you almost want him to hit you so that he *is* touching you again. But he doesn't. You can still taste him on the planes of your mouth.

"Den—"

"*Now* you love me?" Higher pitched than before. "Now, and you still won't—You think you know what I need?"

Shame heats you like the sun. It's selfish to do this to him, to hang on like a weight, like he's yours to take up or discard according to your whims. A tear slides down his cheek, and you decide you can't watch him cry. You can't.

You push forward and take his face in your hands, firmly enough that he can't pull free. "I'm sorry. I'm so … so sorry." *I won't bother you, smother you, guilt-trip you. Tie myself to you any tighter than I already have.* "You can go back now."

He seizes your wrists, holding your hands in place. "Go back where?"

You wipe the moisture from his cheek. The skin beneath his eye is so soft. "To Mike," you sigh, not in relief, not in despair, just the end of a battle. It *is* only a name after all. A heavy, heavy name.

Denny won't stop staring at you. "Mike."

"He's good for you." *He's better than me.* You've never been a destroyer, even when it could help your cause. And, even when it shoves what you want out of your grasp, you can't be a saboteur.

Denny's mouth opens and closes. "I'm not *with* him, Ave." His tone is disdain, frustration. "What are you—"

"But you want to be." You weren't expecting the rise, the edge speeding the words along. You're suddenly weary of this, tired of constant defeat of your own making. "You're in love with him."

"No, I'm not! What the hell do *you* know?"

"I know you miss him. I know you wish you'd never left. That he never let you go." He's said so. You can't forget the lilt of the words as they came out of his mouth.

"You have no idea what I—" Denny throws up his arms and then gets right into your space again. "I miss *being* with him. I miss loving someone like that—no, *being with* someone I love like that, and you—you're—fuck."

There's nothing to say to that.

You thought you had it all figured out, but you just don't know anymore. Somewhere nearby, there's a squeak and a bang, a screen door closing. You can't get your brain out of its stall. It's all fuzz in your ears, and you feel like you've run a mile.

"I just want you to be happy."

"Then stop pushing me away!" Denny yells. "*Fuck* you. You aren't doing me any favors." His voice breaks, and the air rushes out of him with that same shudder when he's coming down, when he's out of words.

But he's not.

"Fuck you," he whimpers, pleading. His fingers curl back into your coat. He's shaking. "Ave ..."

This ... isn't your life. This doesn't happen to you. You don't get what you want, ever, even when you want it this badly. You didn't get your marriage. You didn't get your family back. But Denny's eyes are fixed, liquid and broken, like you broke him. Like you can repair him.

"I don't want to be with *him*." Denny looks ready to kill you. "You tell me to go back to him one more time—"

"Don't," you breathe, trembling in tandem with him, sliding your hands up to grip his elbows. "Don't go. Anywhere. Den, don't—"

"I can't," Denny whispers against your mouth. "I can't go anywhere, I'm—"

He gives up and drags the kiss back again, plying your mouth, bruising your lips. It's surreal and it hurts and it's *wonderful.*

Seconds pass. Could be minutes, for all you know. His body is one long, wiry heave against yours, chest-to-chest, hips jerking restlessly. He's the stoic one, the one who sits still while you fidget, but that's all gone now. A net of live wires has frayed under his skin, and each motion sparks across into you. Maybe you're imagining it. Maybe you just can't think beyond Denny and the way he's pressed to you, thighs and shoulders, mouths on mouths.

"Fucking fags."

Denny wrenches away. Whirls around. Your neighbor, Mr. Abbott, is standing on his porch with the chipping paint and swollen wood, and he's staring knives into your head.

Denny looks back at you, and his body goes stiff as stone. He grips your nape and flips Mr. Abbott off with his other hand. "Shut your fucking mouth!"

Mr. Abbott scowls further. His shoulders hunch, turning his silhouette into a warped troll's. He retreats inside his house and slams the front door.

And Denny's back, breathing your own air back between your lips. "Anything you want, I swear, any—"

You want to kiss him. You want his taste and his heat, the stutter of his lungs. You want him shoving you down even though you're taller, bigger than him. You want him over you, on you, claiming every inch of you.

You want to call yourself his in front of others, to look at other people and know that they could never turn you upside down and right side up again the way he does.

You want him in you. You want him to know he's the only one who's ever been in you. And you want things you can't have—to be his only one in every way—and it hurts, a sweet, bitter ache that you just have to live with.

"I want you." It's the only thing that says it all. The only thing you can manage right now.

"Shit, Ave." He catches your face between his hands again and touches. He traces his thumbs over your lips, bumps his own mouth as he goes. Frames your chin with his palms and strokes the ridges of your cheeks. Your body is doing things you never expected in response to something so simple—overheating, fidgeting, dancing on the edge of outright motion. It's never going to be enough, not even if you have him forever, and your breath escapes too quickly from your lungs. You might be hyperventilating.

You seize his mouth in another kiss, trying to breathe and speak and have him all at the same time. He kisses you back. It's euphoric. It's him, and you're both aware this time.

"I love you, you fucker," Denny gasps out, slamming you into the truck, taking the kiss right out of your grip. "Fucking *months*—" The word snaps in half, its pieces withering in the silence that follows. You hear the hitch, the pain behind it.

You're an idiot for dancing around what's been in front of you for so long.

"Should've said something." But that was your failing, not his.

You push him back long enough to look him in the eye, and then you yank him close again. You'll be bruised from all this shoving, but you don't care. They're his bruises; they're payback for being an idiot, and they'll remind you not to let him end up with someone else by being even worse.

The thought of anyone else's hands on him, of anyone feeling the way his body shakes like this, drives the oxygen out of you so fast that you rock backward. His hands snap down to your sides; again, he holds you up.

"Want you so bad, Den." It's nowhere near what's rampaging through you, trying to contort itself into words.

You have to get him inside the house. The light is too much, as is the noise of the street. It's utter chaos, and Denny is your anchor. You want him where no one can see the look on his face, the abrupt abandon there. Denny, who hides all his emotions, who always moves to stand between you and whatever's threatening. He chooses so often to be the wall, but this time, he's letting his walls crumble. You see so much fragility now.

You've never before thought of Denny as breakable, but he has cracks running all the way through him, and somehow you missed it. For years.

You kiss his cheek, catching the glint under his eye. Salt bursts on your tongue, and you feel so useless, so ashamed and stupid. Why does he want you? Why does he *still* want you?

His hands curl into your jacket and pull you away from the truck. He doesn't stop kissing you, even to walk, and the weight of it bangs against your heart. Get him inside where he's safe. He's not going to hurt again because of you.

You've never wanted to protect anyone like this, like you would destroy the next person who tried to gain something at Denny's expense. Like you actually could do it and not regret a second of it. It's invigorating. It's terrifying.

He tugs you after him up the steps. Your teeth clack, and he grunts. You press him against the wall of the house right next to your rusty mailbox and lick between his lips, anxious to soothe the sting. He arches into you, grabs you tight and drags you forward.

You want to shield him, to finally be the one in the way of all the flak, and you can take it; you're strong enough and, now, aware enough. He breathes sharp, noisy puffs through his nose over your face, kissing you like he'd love to climb inside, steal your warmth.

(In his bed, so many times:

"Too fucking hot," he'd mutter.

In the swelter of summer at night, he'd roll you away, fling back everything but the sheet, and even in your daze, you'd hear the smile in his voice.)

He doesn't taste like cigarettes.

Always, you could taste it, even a single smoke early in the morning, but tonight there's no trace. In his clothes, yes. Of course. But not in him. Not on his tongue or his teeth, not clinging to the corners of his mouth. You breathe his name over his lips, understanding swelling in your innards. It's the one thing you'd change about him if you could, and now he's done it for you—or started to.

How many things about you does he wish you would change? You can think of too many all by yourself, and it breaks your heart, what you must have done to him simply by not seeing. Not noticing anything outside of your own sphere.

In the future, you'll be better. You'll be better at this, at him.

You push him into the door this time and kiss him hard. His mouth tastes like iron. His skin is smooth under your palms, his shirt hem rucked up over your wrists.

He told you once that you were the only one he went home with, to an actual house lived in by an actual person instead of a hotel room or a random bedroom above some party; it's ridiculous, but you believe it utterly because it's Denny, and you don't ever want to find out differently. Even if you do find out, you might just ignore it.

You struggle with the knob digging into the back of his hip, but the door's locked—of course it's locked—and you can't think of where the key is. Just remembering is an immense ordeal. He's invading every thought, every vein. He groans against your mouth, pushes your hips back, and plunges his hands into the pockets of your jeans. He's warm, his fingers separated from your skin by a bare stretch of denim. Arousal spatters through you in tiny bursts, and you buck away, then into him again. He hisses; you like the sound of it.

But he finds the keys and maneuvers them into your hand. His arms come up around your shoulders, and then you're bearing his weight, just you between him and the ground, and you hope to God your neighbor Serena isn't in tonight because there's no way you're ever going to be quiet about this.

The door opens and spills you over the threshold. Denny's foot catches on the frame. He stumbles, grabs hold of your jacket and almost yanks you to the floor on top of him. You catch yourself on the coat rack—came with the house—and pull him back up.

"Okay?" he whispers.

"M'good."

You've never been better, but you'll be even better than this in the next second, and again the second after that. There's no cap to it; Denny will take you up and up and up. Even the person you were going to *marry* never made you feel like this. You're so relieved to know it's possible, that all the stories are really true. Stupid childish dream—here it is. It's so simple.

You lock him close again, and this time, you'll be damned if you let him go, even so he can speak.

He shrugs, hitching at his jacket. You peel it off him, working one arm free and then the other, just the tank top underneath. His throat is a sweaty salt-hollow that you aim to mark up, to suck proof of yourself into, everywhere you can. You barely even recognize yourself: you don't usually like being marked or marking others. It's dirty, an imposition, and too much of a chore. But you can take all the time in the world on Denny, make sure you don't miss an inch and that he knows you're getting everywhere, and maybe that's the most important part.

Fools never get as many chances as you have. If there's a catch, you'll take it and more, as long as it means you still have Denny in your life.

He snakes his hands under your shirt and yanks it upward, popping the buttons free. You've felt his hands on your chest so many times, but this isn't like that at all. How can something so simple as being self-aware make such a difference? Maybe he's touching you differently. You can't analyze, and you don't want to anyway. This is meant to be felt.

He's doing a good job of giving that to you. Denny just knows what you need; you never understood how, but he always has. Even the things you hated him for ... they were all what you needed, and he knew. He gave them all to you, even when you pushed him away, so hard that any normal person would not have come back.

Denny Wyatt is so far beyond normal, you can't quantify it. And that's nice because the day you do is the day you lose its meaning.

You get your mouth on his shoulder, bare skin that tastes like detergent and the mess of that party, and reaction spikes in your belly, a rough plunge of regret that you ever let him walk through those places thinking he wasn't loved or understood. Other people fingering his hair, pulling at his clothing, other people getting in where he didn't want them. You took things for granted. You despair over the thought that he might have let some of them in, those people who don't know him at all, who don't get just how special he is. You want to explain it to them, and you want to keep it from them at the same time. It locks up your muscles. You can't tell which drive is stronger.

"Avery, you all right?" he asks, a scant inch between the two of you, barely enough room for the words to form.

He's out of breath, and you remember out of nowhere him admitting to a severe pollen allergy as a kid, that he sat on the sidelines all thin and reedy, buried in books about the soccer he couldn't play. Maybe he thinks you're having second thoughts. Maybe he doesn't know what to think. That would make two of you.

"You're my best friend," you manage, trying to explain how close you feel, how much you'll do for him, how grateful you are for what he's done for you, how you're responsible for what happened while you were being an idiot. You can't be angry about any of it; you don't have the right.

His chin juts forward. His fingers clench in the hairs at the base of your skull and then smooth immediately. "It's okay. We can stop."

Why is he so accommodating? Doesn't he see you don't deserve it?

You exert yourself, pull him forward, and get your hands beneath his thighs, picking him up off the floor and pressing him to the nearest surface. "I don't want to stop, Den."

Something new breaks between the two of you. Now you're the one struggling to hold your footing while he pushes into you, grips your hair, kisses your thoughts right off the edge of a cliff. You could spend hours on the way he tastes and not care. Just let him kiss you and kiss you until he's finished with you and then do it all over again until you're finished with him. Start over. Repeat. Repeat.

You've always gone into this sort of thing with specific ideas, things you've fantasized about, things you want to try, but you don't want anything particular out of this. There's no clinical edge tonight, no room to peel it apart or analyze. You can't think, and you can't breathe. Denny is Denny. He knows you. He'll give you what you need even if you don't know you need it.

You know enough to understand that you don't want this to happen downstairs, though. Back at his place, you were more than willing, but here, it's all yours, and you want Denny stretched across your bed, limbs sprawled, plenty of room to move him. Let him move you. You want to hold his arms fast up over his head and remove his clothing piece by piece, urge him down onto cool sheets, and you want to be able to lie down when you're done, with a pillow and blankets that smell like the two of you together.

It's never been awkward, sleeping with Denny. He never kicks you out when you're done, and you know he kicks others out or leaves himself. Might as well be a friend staying over, only you just had sex, and it's just another thing you do: argue, eat, fuck, watch TV.

Denny usually talks in bed afterward, sucks on the end of an unlit cigarette, and complains about the shop's spotty inventory, the customers who don't give a shit that there's a living, breathing human working on their precious cars. He tells jokes he learned from his coworker Gina, and he asks whether you've heard from your family. When he sleeps, he sleeps—there's nothing extra in it—and when he wakes up, he's ready to start anew. A bed is a bed, but once it's served its function, Denny will climb out and move on.

He's never been one to cuddle, but then you've never given him reason to. Tonight, that will change.

You nudge him around the couch, and he stumbles, catching himself with one hand. You don't have a big place, but you could walk it blind, and it's easy to right him, to keep going down the hallway to your bedroom. Halfway there, he releases your mouth and bends to your throat instead. His teeth catch at the tender skin over your collarbone. You shiver.

Down the hall—feels longer than it is—and then to your room.

You're simultaneously uneasy and okay with the mess. Denny's seen it. Hell, he probably helped make it. He practically lives at your place some weeks, when you're both too lazy to get him home. But you haven't cleaned in weeks either, and now, you realize you can't remember the last time he was over for more than a *Hey, let's go, car's running.*

Maybe some part of you refused to clean because it mourned his absence and couldn't be sure when that would be rectified.

The bed isn't made, and you fumble around until you can pull the quilt out of the way. It's unwieldy; you curse, trying to shift it onehanded. Denny takes your chin in his fingers, turns your mouth to his again and silences you, humming against your lips. You can't control the sound you make.

You want to touch him all over. Fuck all this damn clothing. Why is it still here?

The tang of his sweat beats like a drum over your tongue. You thrust your hips in time, push him onto the bed and fit yourself to him, and he's just—it works, all of it. His body is so familiar, it hurts.

"God, Den." It's amazing you can get any sound out at all.

He smells like he always has—a million memories every time you inhale. Your entire friendship assaults you at once, and it's fascinating, giddy. A roller coaster you've ridden time and time again, but it never gets old. You push up into him, roll your hips down, breathe him in.

He rears back suddenly. Your nose bumps the underside of his chin.

"Ave."

It's not desire this time but a different kind of vulnerability. You back off, with an effort. He's looking up at you, eyes wide.

"This." His throat moves when he swallows, and his fingers clench over your side. "This just going to be tonight? Or ..."

You can only stare back and wait. He swallows again, a dry click.

Denny's life, as far as you know it, has been nothing but a series of outstanding disappointments. He plays it all very close to the chest, and he's never tried to outdo you in the pity party department. Denny's never held one for himself at all, while you've indulged in several. But then, you've never been repeatedly kicked in the chest by your best friend, leaving you with a habit of standing against walls rather than showing anyone your back. You've never been thrown out of your house by a parent, and even if that parent did let Denny back in a few months later, you've never been viciously ignored like he was, your entire existence utterly denied by everyone in the house. You've never been able to count your friends on one hand, let alone one finger. Denny is your closest friend, but he's not your only friend. You've tried not to think about it. You thrive on the times when the two of you are alone—other people just make things complicated—but you can't say the same for him.

If the situation were reversed, you wouldn't be willing to risk him for a single night, no matter how good it could be. In the end though, desperation might drive you to it, and you can see in Denny's face how thinly stretched he is. Months of reaching for an acknowledgment you were sure would never come, and finally, here it is. You'd take hold of it while you could. But you'd know, even as you reached, that the world would pull it even further from your grasp come morning.

Just tonight?

"No, I don't want it to be."

You don't deserve him, but you *need* him. More than that, you want him to want you. If he doesn't—

"Den." It's a prayer, the way his name slips off your tongue. "If ... Denny, what do you want it to be?"

He's not going to answer. It's shocking how clearly you can read him tonight.

You nuzzle at his mouth and kiss him, slick, deep, and then you just say it. "I don't want just tonight. I want you."

Should have said you loved him. You want the life of him, not just his body. You want to know him through and through. You want years, not fucks. A soul mate, not simply a lover. You're abruptly a stuttering romantic when it comes to Denny, but you can't say it aloud.

"Okay," he breathes and pushes up into you, coiled with heat and fervor, just shooting it out for everyone to see.

Denny never lets down his guard, but here he is. The sacrifice is complete. There's nothing left behind. You gather him up. Thank God you're the only one who can understand it for what it is. Thank God twice that you would never take advantage of it like some people might—like some people have? An ugly thought, and you don't want to know if it's true. If it is, you'll have to hurt someone, and he'll never give you a name even if they scarred him.

There are so many layers. He's a puzzle, and if you take him apart, you need to be able to put him back exactly as you found him. Whether he ends up wanting that or not, you have to be able to do it.

If you weren't so sure of how you felt about him, how you'll feel about him in a week, a month, a year, *ten* years, you'd stop this right now.

The thing is, Denny will let you have tonight. He'll do it, no matter what reasons you give him. Whether you let him stay in the morning or you get up and leave yourself, it makes no difference to the next few hours. His walls are already down, and he's not putting them back up. You decide right there that, whatever he thinks might happen, you are going to prove you've earned every millimeter of the ground you've gained.

He struggles up, pulls himself into your lap, and wraps his legs round your waist. It's a familiar position; you've been on the reverse end of it, too. But you're still clothed, and that's weirdly intimate—the knowledge that you can take your time in getting to all the rest. Right now, it's okay if there are off-white shirts and ribbed tank tops and cotton boxers between you; it's early, and the point tonight isn't to get off. The point is to do this well. It doesn't even matter if he doesn't reciprocate and get you off too. If getting him to the apex again and again for the next twelve hours will keep him from that dark place, from worrying about what happens after, you'll do it without hesitation.

Denny's your standard candle, the light you base everything on, the foundation for all the calculations you've made in the past nine years, and you didn't even realize it. Never thought of it that way at all.

It's a lot to digest in the stretch of only two seconds.

Denny's body is all unchecked motion against yours. The denim of his jeans is thin and soft from wear; he's had these same jeans for ages, he wears them every week. But, against your body, it's all coarse, tingling motion; you itch to pull away what separates the two of you and feel even more of him. Sate this ache.

What puzzles you is that you've been closer than this with him before. You've been naked together—hell, inside him, as close to him as you could ever get—and this still feels uncharted, like this night will be different. New.

Fear slips in. What if it's not new enough? What if this is a disappointment to him? You know each other so well that there can't possibly be anything special about sex anymore.

You push it down, but it proves to be too much, and you pull out of the next kiss to get some oxygen into your lungs. Your vision swims, but he's looking at you, assessing what has gone wrong.

What comes out of your mouth isn't about him at all. "What if I'm not ... Den, you and me ..."

What if Den's the one disappointed?

You gesture between the two of you, and your hand feels disturbingly cold now that it's no longer in contact with his body. You're so embarrassed, and half of it is because you know you shouldn't be.

"We've already—" You stop.

His gaze flicks back and forth between your eyes, studying. He's figuring you out like he always has, and you wish he couldn't see it all. He takes your face in his hands. Your cheeks flush hot under his palms.

"It's going to be fine, Avery."

He's so sure.

You swallow, and his thumb brushes your face.

You've always believed Denny. Right from that first moment—*"You shouldn't drink the punch at these things"*—whatever he says, there's something in you that nods and replies, *Yes, you're absolutely right.*

And that's the end of it.

As far as you know, he's never lied to you. But the point is that you've never questioned, never felt the need. You've disagreed—who doesn't disagree every once in a while?—but doubting Denny's words, his belief in what he's saying? It's not how you're wired.

So, when he says it'll be fine, your fear gives up and slides away. You nod, and he guides you down to the bed again.

Kissing Denny isn't sweet. You can tell immediately that he's not in the mood for that. He *wants* you. Every kiss tugs at you, a demand, yet he doesn't stop the kissing and move on. He strokes the roof of your mouth with his tongue, lingers on the rim of your lips, nips with his teeth. Your mouth is going to be so sore when he's done, before he's done, even. It's been a long time since you felt so bruised, and while you've never been into pain during sex, this is the good sort of ache, the kind that will remind you for days of what you did, make you remember it in bright neon.

Suddenly, you're thinking of the aftermath, being with Denny like this and then waking up to a new day. You yank him close, and he grunts but doesn't move away. Just pulls you down on top of him, hooks a leg over yours, and cinches your hips tight to his. He drags your shirt over your head, works it free of your arms, and then you're leaning over him, hands on either side of his shoulders, looking into his eyes.

He cups your nape. Grips and relaxes. His lips purse, as though he's trying hard to keep them closed.

You get your fingers under his tank top and bare his stomach, tracking each breath as he draws it. He's not overtly muscular, never succumbed to the need to prove his power to others, like you did. But it's all there underneath.

Denny pushes up onto his elbows and watches your hands roam over his skin. He shudders when you trip across his ribs, and you recall flooring him with a well-placed pinch, followed by his bark of laughter. You remember the full-body cringe as he gave up the secret to getting anything you ever wanted out of him. He's ticklish. Really ticklish.

His eyes are dark, the pupils swallowing the brown. His lashes are long, like most men's.

You bunch his shirt up under his arms. He's got a tattoo of a star, but not just any star. This star looks like something from the Hubble photographs, rich blues and misty grays with sharp flares rearing from its surface. Inner light. It's only a few years old, and you remember the sound he made, the expression that stuck on his face while the tattoo artist buzzed her way through the design, her tongue quirked at the corner of her mouth. You remember the jerk of Denny's hand on the armrest, almost reaching for yours.

"Blue supergiant," he said after.

"It glows," you said. "Or seems to."

The star sits above his left nipple. He always tells you it's not done, that he wants to add more, a whole constellation down his side and around to his back. He hasn't touched it since the initial job though, and you trace the path it would have taken with your fingertips—under his arm, a trail along his side toward his spine.

He shifts his weight, and you hold his gaze for as long as you can, until you touch your mouth to the star. His hips twitch upward once.

"Get this off." You pull at his tank top.

He removes it, drops it somewhere to your left and returns to you, sweeping his hands up and down your sides. You've never been ticklish like him, but his touch makes your calves tingle. If you were standing, your knees would buckle.

You don't get emotional with your lovers. Neither does he. But something has fallen apart inside him. His face, his eyes, the very way he lies against the mattress—it's all open. The arch of his throat invites; his whole body seems to rise toward you.

What do you look like to him? You hope to God he understands what he's done to you because you have no idea how to reverse it, how to explain it if he asks.

His belt is cheap black leather, rubbed rough under the buckle, and his belly heaves when you weave the end of it back through the bracket and pull it loose. His muscles contort, his navel dipping inward above the hair that disappears into his jeans. You struggle with the top button, but the zipper comes down cleanly, and his skin goes hot against your fingers. Patches of red darken his sides, and you look up in time to see him drop his head back, eyes fixed foggily upward. His throat works. Then, he cranes his neck and looks down at you, biting his lip. His teeth are white against ruddy skin.

You flip your own belt open and surge up, tucking your hand down the front of his pants. Your mouth meets his, and you feel his first tremble through the kiss, the sharp arch of his hips. His hand wriggles between you, locks around your wrist, but he doesn't stop you. He's just there, with you, riding it as silently as he can. You can't hold the kiss; he exhales against your mouth, shaky. His head jumps like he can't keep still, and you lean your weight down onto him to watch, fascinated.

The hand still at your neck sneaks into your hair and tenses in rhythm with your movements. You don't want him to come like this—he's not even undressed yet—but it's too huge, seeing him slide higher and higher with each roll of your hips, the chafe of denim across your hand and the damp pocketed heat where you're holding him. His zipper gnaws at your knuckles, at his flesh, and he hisses. Thrusts upward.

You let go.

He grabs on to you so quickly that you startle.

You press him back. "It's okay, Den. It's—"

"Wait," he says.

But now he's out of breath, holding on to you like you might leave him here in the middle of your bed. He slowly lets go, his hands drifting down your shoulders.

He looks so *young*.

You bump his nose with yours and tell him again: "It's okay." But your voice cracks.

He's not supposed to be the vulnerable one. He's left it to you for so long, always been there to prop you up when you stumbled sideways, push you back onto the road in the right direction. You're not sure you can do the same—hold him steady when he's not. You'll do it wrong, make his fall even harder.

Denny's fingers glide over yours where they rest on his chest. Then he twists to the side, reaching for your bedside table drawer. He pulls out a handful of condoms and lube. Not only does he know exactly where everything is, but he also doesn't hesitate to find it.

If there is ever control wanting, Denny steps in and takes it up as easily as a mantle. Then, later, he confides that he was scared out of his mind—*had no idea what I was doing, man.*

You don't usually believe him, but you've been wrong about a lot of things.

It, this, is so very much him that you stall out, your hand clenched into a fist over his sternum. He sinks down again on the bed. You're not looking at his face, rather at the supplies in his grip, but you know he's watching you, taking it all in. You splay your hand flat on his chest again and ease one of the condoms free. His pulse jumps where you touch; his skin is extraordinarily hot.

When you go for his pants again, you make sure to look him in the eye. He's staring placidly back, but it's a front; underneath, he's edging right out of his skin, struggling not to move and give himself away. Maybe he's afraid that, if he lets go, you'll spook and run, recall that this is so far beyond where you've both been for the past nine years. He knows fear is contagious. He'll never let on if he's already been ensnared by it.

Does he realize you can already see it in him, that you know him so well, you can read right through to the thoughts hanging behind his eyes? All it took was one final nudge to open the door. And, if he has no clue that you know him like this, then—

You shake your head. Shake it away. It smarts.

You pull his pants down, and he plants his shoulders, bows up off the mattress and lets you undress him. Boxers and belt and jeans come away, and you drop them off the edge of the bed.

He's pretty pale—burns too easily and doesn't often go out in the sun. His eyes stray up and down, as though he's never really looked at you. But he's seen you in every way imaginable.

Denny raises his knee and bumps you with it. God, how can one person be two such opposing forces at once? He's collected, and he's also juddering right out of his skin, and you're witnessing *both*.

But he's moving, too—hauling himself upright, reaching for your belt. He unsnaps and unzips everything with the certainty you've come to expect from him. It's a relief to see it again. His forearms flex as he works your belt free and lays it aside—doesn't toss it like you did, just sets it down and moves on to the next thing. He gets your pants partway over your hips and stops to mouth your jaw—a brief touch. And again. You close your eyes at the flicker of his tongue.

It goes on for long enough that you decide he's waiting for you.

It's hard to tell what motivates the hesitance. His eyes are hooded now as well as aroused, and he won't quite look at you. You take his chin in your hand and kiss him, awkward as you struggle out of your clothing.

His taste sparks across your tongue again, and soon you've got nothing between you but space.

His hands come to rest on your thighs, right at the crease of your hips. He snakes forward and lips another tiny kiss. Grips your wrist and pulls you in.

You shake at the full-body contact, at the feeling of the two of you breathing in counterpoint. Everything spikes, bright and sharp. Time drags. He urges you further down, bracketing you with his thighs. You grab his wrists and force him still again, bury your face in his throat and hold on. Drown yourself in his smell. There's something foreign under your palm; you've crushed a packet of lube between your hand and his arm.

He's nodding before you even formulate the question, his chin bumping the top of your head. "Do it."

The pause after jolts you into motion. You track down his body, losing the lube at his hip, groping until you find it in the sheets. You tear it open, and then you're there, fingertips poised and slick. Denny's entire frame quakes, little shivers you want to follow with your mouth, if you could just figure out where they began.

He's warm, yielding when you push in. The muscles of his thigh tense against your arm. He bumps your chin up and kisses you, makes you forget to worry about what you're doing and how you're doing it. You're incredibly, ridiculously thankful.

He's the one who handles the condom—Denny's always been good at multitasking—gets it on you, and waits with his lips pressed firmly to your forehead while you hold yourself rigid, trying to catch up. You're not sure if he's truly ready when he hitches his hips, urging you up and into him; you try to ask if it's okay, but his legs cinch around you, and it's all blown away. You can't string two letters together, never mind words. It's all heat, a sinuous slide, clenching muscle.

He gets you seated, and then he holds still, hands tight around your biceps, waiting.

"Den?"

You don't have the faculty to kiss him properly, just lips touching down again and again on anything you can reach, your breaths skittering across each other, but you need to kiss him; you don't want to resist it. He bucks a little, adjusting his position, and raises his head as though he's going to sit up. He drops back instead with a groan. His hand finds your nape again. He loves touching you there; he does it even when you aren't having sex. Day to day, he grips you and gives you a shake, like he's jiggling your thoughts back into place. Here, in the dark with the room's air thickening around you, it works just the same.

You open your eyes fully and look down into his.

Maybe he still thinks this is a one-off. Maybe he's not thinking at all, just moving, getting you where he thinks *you* need to be. Maybe he has shut his thoughts down because he can't think about this as it happens. For you, everything's almost too much. You wish you could think, analyze all of this. Get it absolutely right for him.

God, you *love* him. So, so ...

You move, and he utters a broken sound, eyes rolling back, chin tilting up, baring his throat for your mouth. You take advantage, laving every bit of skin you can reach. It takes coordination, but it's not as hard as all that, or maybe you're just not overthinking it anymore. You know his body and how to move him, and you find yourself just going for it, reaching down, repositioning his hips, bracing an arm under his back, working the angle until his panting becomes mere sound, smashed words. His fingers dig bruises you'll see tomorrow all over your body. You wait until he's sucking air between his teeth, and then you pull upright, lean back, and drag his hips up over your thighs. Snug him tightly against you.

A violent current skims his muscles. In your mind, you see his toes curling behind you. His hand scrabbles across the sheets, clenching handfuls so tightly, you're sure that, if not for the fabric in the way, his palms would be bleeding. His face contorts, hovering somewhere between agony and bliss, so you move again—your body does it on its own, knows him so damn well—and you thrust deep and long, not pulling out much, relentlessly right up inside him, bringing him just short of the top and keeping him there.

You're about to come. But Denny's going to come first; you're determined. If you time it right, he won't even be able to make a sound. It'll last so long, and then you'll set him off again when you finish. He'll be *beautiful* as he tries to ride it, shaking and panting and going completely ragged until it's well over.

You shudder forward and mouth the underside of his chin, reaching down at the same time, pulling him off. Only two strokes and he's gone, tightening all around you, thighs squeezing at your hips, chin bucking down, knocking your nose, mouth slack even as his jaw cracks. He'll never remember it—hitting you with his chin—but you will, and you'll recall the hiss of breath as it exploded out of him and the way he went taut, every inch.

It's not disappointing at all. And that's all you have time to think before you follow him, collapsing under the orgasm, catching yourself against his chest, heat and waves of near pain, scratching an itch that sits far too deep. It coils in your belly and surges out, shooting up your spine, down the backs of your legs. Something's gripping you too tightly, but you can't think, can't sort it out—

And then the release.

You breathe hard, face pressed to Denny's sweaty chest, and it's over.

It's over.

His name runs through your mind on a loop; you might be saying it aloud. Your ears hum. He strokes fingers down your back, but it feels like his whole hand, several hands. Every nerve ending jolts, and you can't make sense of what you're feeling. Except, you're still inside him. You know every tremor of his body, too.

"You okay?" He has to say it three times before you answer. The third time is just a single syllable, "'Kay?" as though he can no longer exert the energy.

You nod into his chest. Your nose is smashed and sore, but the taste of him settles back on your tongue when you inhale, and you don't want to move.

You should ask him how he is. Too complicated. He hasn't moved, pushed you off, or even hinted that you should take the initiative. How many times have you been in his bed, just trying to breathe again? But this is the first time like this. Usually, you get up, get right off of him or he right off of you, and you get on with things. You've never stayed still and listened to his heartbeat, as though it might leap out of his body and into yours.

You sort of want it to.

You need to speak, your mind sluggishly suggests.

This requires talking about what happened, not the stupid stuff you two usually talk about afterward—assholes wrecking their chances at the playoffs or who you think is fucking whom at your job or the hot little roadster that came into Denny's shop the other day. You just don't know what to say that you haven't already said—that you love him, that this is what you wanted. *Want.* Saying it again isn't going to make it any truer, but maybe saying it again is what you have to do. You're not sure.

It takes effort to get your arms back in order, but finally, you push up. The words you were planning vanish. Denny looks back, taking in every detail, and then he tucks your hair away from your forehead. You feel the slide of your own sweat.

"Hey," he says. *Hey*, and nothing else. His lips flash up at the corners, but the smile disappears just as fast.

You become aware all over again of the tension of his body around you, the fact that he hasn't asked you to move, but this can't be comfortable for him.

Still. You reach up and cup his chin. Kiss his mouth. He doesn't respond, but then he's kissing you back, and it's different from before, not frantic or quick or even lingering. It's unhurried. Tender, deliberate. There's something under it, like he doesn't want to end it. Doesn't want to let it go.

Eventually, it has to end, and you reach down, carefully pull out of him, and get up on your hands and knees. Your back aches; you wonder how his feels. Your muscles are heavier than ever, like they've all been twisted up and you're only now sorting them back into order. You get rid of the condom, clean him up a little with the sheet, and breathe like you spent the last three days running. Even easing down onto your side takes effort, and you groan. His hand finds your shoulder and guides you down, though there would be little he could do if you fell off the bed or ... well, did anything really.

As you lie there trying to calm your breathing, he rubs his palm up and down your arm. It's soothing. But your chest hurts. That's what he's aiming for; he expects you to fall apart in a bad way over this, and he's already trying to keep you together.

Your eyes are closed when his lips touch your face, just below your temple where your skin is cooling.

It could be the brush of a finger through your bangs or maybe just the movement of air as he speaks. "Thank you."

Oh God, for what? For giving him something when your heart wasn't really in it? Is that what he's thinking?

You search out his hand and panic when you can't find it. Then, suddenly, there it is, and you latch on, entwine your fingers, and hold him still, and look down to make sure. It makes sense in your mind: *don't let him move until he gets it.*

"No. Don't *thank* me, Den. Don't."

His face is still flushed, a sheen over his forehead, cheeks, down his throat where his pulse visibly thrums. He opens his mouth, but you cut him off, kiss him quiet, hold him there, feeling your way back into this and guiding him along behind you. You sense him succumbing, muscles ticking loose in increments. If you can kiss him for long enough, he'll—

He sighs and drops out of it but doesn't pull away. Just lies there, breathing. Each huff touches your mouth. You use the opportunity to study him.

You long to give him something, to put weight back on his end of the scales. He's taken so much off tonight and handed it to you. There's only one thing you can think of, maybe something he never thought about again after that first night when you asked him to show sex to you. You were just twenty.

"Don't want it to be bad. Don't want it to hurt. You know."

Such a long damn time ago.

The second you decide on your course of action, it feels trivial. What does Denny care? But that's the wrong voice talking, trying to gain back the ground it's lost tonight, and the point is that *you* care. You care about this, and he'll see that and understand.

"You know, you're the only one who's ever—" You gesture down toward your body. Your nakedness feels so very apparent. You don't look at him, and you don't finish the sentence.

"What?" He shifts even closer. "Ever what?"

All the descriptions seem so vulgar. Only ever fucked you? Penetrated you? That's just stupid. As far as you know, you haven't actually made love until tonight, and that suspicion has you all shaky, unsure of who you *are*, let alone whether or not you can handle it. You can't use the phrase *made love* because that could go either way. On your end, it's true. That's all you can be sure of. You can't speak plainly to Denny anymore; you have to talk in *almosts* and euphemisms, make hand signals at your own body like you're still in grade school, blushing before judgmental classmates.

"Been in me."

His silence shortens your breath. You don't know what your other lovers thought about it, about you, but you know now that it never mattered with them anyway. It does matter with Denny. What he thinks of you, whether he was right or wrong about you, whether he wanted to be and whether it mattered to him.

He disentangles your hands and touches your cheek. The line of each finger tracks cool against your flaming skin. Denny's thumb skips across your lips.

"Okay," he whispers. "It's okay."

Not an answer at all, and it still fills up the hole of your admission.

Denny swallows and lifts his chin. For a second, he looks like a kid, overwhelmed and trying to deal. But underneath it, he's still Den, ready to move mountains for you.

He draws you closer. You can't *get* any closer.

"Am I really?" He sounds bewildered.

Embarrassment hits—not at what you said, but at how he responded, that he can be this tender when you've always been so crass.

"Ye—" Your voice hasn't fractured like this in years. You clear your throat and look away. "Yeah. Really."

He taps your cheek, guiding your attention back around. "How come?"

You don't really know. Because you trusted him, and you didn't want to screw up with anyone else later on. Because when he said he was clean, you believed him, just in case condoms weren't all they were cracked up to be. Because you wanted to practice. Of course, those are reasons. But if that had been all it was, you would have gone ahead and let someone else do it after. It never felt right, though, and you figured, okay, you just needed to be more comfortable with it before you tried with someone else. And then it never happened with someone else, and now, you're glad.

"Just didn't want to, I guess. With anyone else."

Right now, Denny could make a crack about being *that good*, ruining him for everyone else, and it would not only be true, it would be in character. But this isn't that Denny—the one goofing off at parties, the one who tried to impress a sixteen-year-old valiantly vomiting onto a stranger's lawn. This is the Denny who knows what it's like to have a name that sounds too old for his body, the one you trusted to teach you about sex with a guy in the first place, and this Denny doesn't fuck around with the important stuff.

He doesn't say anything at all; instead, he pushes up onto his elbow, kisses the backs of your knuckles, and holds them to his mouth. When he sinks back down, he rests his chin on your chest. Looks at you. Sometimes, you don't like the way he stares. It's as though he can see everything you're hiding, hear you confessing it out loud. Now, it's him considering you, taking you in. It's nice to be looked at like that. You look back.

You picture others, but all the details have been sucked out of the motif, and they're only flimsy facsimiles of what attracts you. Shells, nothing inside to draw you in. You can't imagine being with them now.

Eventually, Denny's eyes drop, and he sighs, pillows his cheek where his chin was. Then he rolls over and aligns himself against your flank. You both look up at the ceiling, as though you're outside, stargazing. Your breathing is out of sync. You're not sure what he's feeling right now, but you're still coming down, *still* fighting the muscle spasms that accompanied your orgasm and the admission afterward. You're going to need a few minutes, a few hours maybe. Whatever. He's not leaving until you're ready.

You wonder if he knows that yet.

"Need a smoke," Denny drawls.

"No." It's out before you think.

He lifts his head and stares at the hand you've snapped around his wrist.

You've overstepped, taken one too many liberties at last. It's not like you own him. Your stomach twists.

He kisses you again, sweet and thorough. "Said I need one, Ave." He rests his temple against yours. "Not that I'm gonna have one."

You turn your head until your cheek touches his. There's so much you'd like to say, but not all of it needs to be said. It's nerves, yours and his, always playing off each other when your bodies are in the same space. It has manifested in cars driven too fast, people danced with too closely, tight fists and seething words where a glare would have been enough. But all of that feels old and worn, the concerns of an age ago when you didn't know you had Denny's heart. You certainly didn't understand that he already had yours.

"Stay here. Today." You slide your hand up his arm, gripping higher, holding him close. "Just."

He's already nodding, kissing the side of your mouth. "Yeah, if you want me to."

You turn into the kiss and take control of it to show him how much you want that. If he's not going to listen to words—after all, you've given him plenty of reasons to question yours in the years you've known each other—then you'll just have to speak in other ways until he can't ignore what's being said any longer.

Your hand is on his chest again, and even though you're not looking, you know it's resting atop his tattoo. His star. You're holding the star in your palm, containing it and releasing its power at the same time, and underneath it, always, beats the steady rhythm of Denny's heart.

Acknowledgements

MANY, MANY THANKS... I'm always terrified I will forget someone!

First, thank you to Saritza, my agent. This is the first manuscript of mine that you ever read, Sary! And from the moment you read the first draft, you have tirelessly supported and assisted me in my endeavors to publish it, and I am heartily grateful.

Thank you to Melanie, to Darcy, to Christine, and to Diana and her daughter: readers, all, who provided much helpful feedback and commentary. Prolific thanks go to lyric, who is a generous fount of knowledge in maneuvering the world of internet publishing.

Many thanks, also, to the crew at Draft2Digital, to Regina for her sublime cover art, and to Jovana for editing.

To all the fantastic people who have contacted me since I started posting my work publicly: You are too many to name here, but your incredible enthusiasm for my writing has been a driving force behind what I've accomplished.

And last but *never* least, thank you from the bottom of my heart to my parents De and Steve, and to my sister Berit, for your love, strength, and enthusiasm as I chase my dream.

Best Lesbian Erotica of the Year, Volume 5

An anthology edited by
Sinclair Sexsmith

Short Story: The Estranged

Testing the boundaries of pleasure and pain... To be so full of longing you ache for release... Coming to climax without a single touch.

The fifth volume of the Best Lesbian Erotica of the Year anthology series explores and expands on the very definition of eroticism with a diverse mix of queer, non-binary, trans, and polyamorous #ownvoices that will have you quivering with delight and wondering what more you can explore—no matter how you identify. More than just steamy sex stories, this volume offers the quiet sexuality of emotional security, the overwhelming thrill of discovering something new, and a tale for every taste—from vanilla to kink to strap-ons and sodomy.

Now more than ever, it is crucial to see unique, underrepresented viewpoints across the literary spectrum. Award-winning author and editor Sinclair Sexsmith delivers in an anthology that is both tender and tantalizing, emotional and evocative.

· · · · ·

Coming soon from Cleis Press

Secrets of Neverwood

An anthology about found family by
G.B. Lindsey
Diana Copland
Libby Drew

• • • •

Three foster brothers are called home to Neverwood, the stately Pacific Northwest mansion of their youth. They have nothing in common but a promise to Audrey, the woman they all called mother—that upon her death, they would restore the house and preserve it as a home for troubled boys.

But going home is never easy.

Cal struggles to recover from past heartbreak, while Danny fears his mistakes are too big to overcome. Devon believes he may never break down the barriers that separate him from honest emotion.

On the path to brotherhood, they discover the old mansion holds more than dusty furniture and secret passageways. Audrey's spirit still walks its halls, intent on guiding "her boys" toward true love, and an old mystery stirs up a new danger—one that could cost the men far more than just the house.

• • • •

Available at Carina Press

Condoms and Hot Tubs Don't Mix: An Anthology of Awkward Sexcapades

Edited by
Jennie Jarvis
Leslie Salas
Catherine Carson

. . . .

Short Story: Laid Over

. . . .

Real sex isn't as graceful and glamorous as romance novels and pornography often portray. Real sex is learning you have a latex allergy while you lose your virginity. And so, the stories, essays, poems, and comics in Condoms and Hot Tubs Don't Mix offer realistic sex scenes to counter the overly coercive and falsely romantic scenes portrayed by books, films, and TV shows.

. . . .

Available at Beating Windward Press

Don't miss out!

Visit the website below and you can sign up to receive emails whenever G.B. Lindsey publishes a new book. There's no charge and no obligation.

https://books2read.com/r/B-A-JDGL-LYUGB

BOOKS 2 READ

Connecting independent readers to independent writers.

About the Author

G. B. Lindsey was born and raised in California. Her first love has always been writing: as a child, she cultivated such diverse goals as becoming "a cowgirl and a writer" or "a paleontologist and a writer." Aside from her salacious affair with the horror genre, she loves to write sci-fi, romance, historical fiction, and short stories. Other hobbies include playing the piano, voracious reading, the occasional period drama movie night, and devouring scary films. She has a Master of Arts in Creative Writing from Newcastle upon Tyne, and now lives with her cat in California.

Read more at https://www.gblindsey.com/.